The Captain's Return

by Warren Hussey Bouton

Illustrated by Barbara Kauffmann Locke

Hither Creek Press
Short Hills, New Jersey

*This book is dedicated to
Shadrach, Sadie and Reggie,
and to all loved ones
past and present.*

CHAPTER

1

"Ben, would you please pipe down for a minute. We need to hear the weather forecast."

I looked up from my breakfast cereal and could tell that Dad was serious. There was just a little bit of an edge to his voice and the look in his eyes told me it was time to be quiet.

There we were, enjoying another summer vacation at the family cottage in Madaket. The weather had been great with lots of sun and gentle breezes off the water but now the clouds were starting to build, the wind was beginning to blow, and the island was being threatened by a hurricane.

"The National Weather Service has issued a hurricane warning for the Cape and the islands," the weatherman announced. "Projections show that Hurricane Bob will pass directly over Nantucket by late morning with steady winds of 85 miles per hour. All residents of low-lying areas should proceed immediately to emergency shelters. Stay tuned for the latest information."

"What should we do?" Mom, Sarah and I all gasped at once, looking at Dad.

He sat and looked out the window for a minute, and then said, "I don't think we have much to worry about. This house has ridden out worse storms than this one. I think it'll be fun to stay and watch it from here!"

Fun? I knew my father had a really
strange sense of humor, but this was a bit too
much even for me.

The family cottage was right on the water overlooking Madaket harbor. It was a tiny house with just two small bedrooms, a kitchen with a table to eat at, and a front room with a built-in couch, a bed that doubled as a sofa, and a bunch of old chairs. There was a porch on one side, an outside shower and, except for the bathroom that was the size of a tiny closet, that was about it. My great-grandfather had built the cottage, and this little piece of heaven was sacred ground to my family. It was a fantastic place to watch sunsets and to enjoy the beach, but I wasn't too sure that experiencing a hurricane in it was the best thing to do. And the look on Sarah's and Mom's faces made me believe that I wasn't the only one who was thinking that way.

CHAPTER 2

"Come on," Dad said. "Whether we stay or go into town, we need to bring in the outside furniture, the grill, and anything else the wind might toss around. So let's get to it."

Outside, it was a beehive of activity. People who kept their boats moored in the small harbor were quickly pulling their anchors and heading to the boat launch, where there was a line of trucks and SUVs with trailers waiting to carry their boats to safety. Our neighbors were all out and about making sure that everything that might blow away was safely secured or carried inside. As Sarah, Dad, and I scampered about grabbing lawn chairs, clam rakes, and beach umbrellas and putting them in the garage, the wind was already beginning to get strong. Once, a gust of wind almost knocked me off my feet and I had to lean into it just to keep my balance.

"I think we've got everything," Dad finally called as he looked around the corner of the house. "Let's get inside."

We scrambled into the cottage and shut the door behind us. I couldn't believe how quiet it was in the house. Outside, the wind whipping our ears had been almost deafening, but inside our sturdy little cottage everything seemed peaceful...until we looked out the window. I was beginning to think that Dad was right about staying.

"Dad," Sarah said with a worried tone. "don't you think we should go into town so we're away from the water?"

"Don't be silly. We're perfectly safe. There is no reason to panic. We'll watch the storm from right here. No problem."

No sooner had my father spoken those words than a loudspeaker boomed: "This is the Nantucket Police Department. We are evacuating all low-lying beach areas. Please proceed as soon as possible to town. If you do not have family or friends to stay with, the high school has been designated as an emergency shelter. A hurricane warning is in effect. Please leave as soon as possible."

With that, Mom looked at my father and

said, "Right, dear, no problem! No problem at all. Give me the keys to the Jeep. We're going to town."

CHAPTER 3

"Grandma, Grandpa, did you hear? There's a hurricane coming!" I screamed as my big sister and I ran through the kitchen door of my grandparents' house in town. Mom, Dad, and our golden retriever, Sadie, quickly followed us into the kitchen.

"Oh yes. We've heard all right," my grandmother answered. "Grandpa has already collected everything outside that the wind might carry away and stowed it in the workshop or the garage. I've managed to find plenty of candles and flashlights in case the power goes out. We're ready and waiting. You know, in the old days we didn't know so far in advance that a hurricane was coming. We just watched the barometer drop and knew we were in for a storm. Now, with all these weather forecasters and their computers, all the surprise has been taken out of it."

Then Grandma got a funny smile on her face; she stooped down and whispered into our ears, "Can I tell you a secret?"

"Sure!" Sarah and I whispered back as we moved closer to Grandma to hear what she had to say.

"I'm looking forward to it! We haven't had a good hurricane for a long time!"

I could hardly believe my ears. Grandma

was looking forward to a hurricane! I really shouldn't have been surprised. Grandma and Grandpa had lived on Nantucket their whole lives. They were used to riding out storms in their creaky old house. Sarah and I had visited with them a lot over the years and we had kind of gotten used to the way the house squeaked and groaned with the changing of the weather. But the one thing we had never gotten comfortable with were the ghosts that called this old house home! It seemed as if every time we came for a visit we ran into another spooky ancestor. Of course, the worst ghost of all was an angry old whaling captain named Ichabod Paddack. We'd had more than one scary adventure with him, and I didn't want another one. I could take a hurricane any day, but Captain Paddack? I'd had enough of him!

Unfortunately for Sarah and me, the hurricane was soon to become the least of our worries.

CHAPTER 4

"Well, look who's here—my little Suzie-Q and Jesse James!" Grandpa boomed as he came in, shaking the water from his raincoat. Grandpa was always calling us by funny names. He liked to tease us by pretending to forget who we were. "The storm is coming fast now. Just look at how the weeping willow in the backyard is bending over."

Sarah and I ran to the window and were amazed to see the branches of the willow tree whipping in the wind. The rain from Hurricane

14

Bob had started and was now coming down in sheets.

"I think we might as well settle in for a while," Mom said as all the lights in the kitchen suddenly went out. "Well—there goes the electricity. Let's break out the books and the games. I don't think we're going anywhere until this storm is over."

And boy, was Mom ever right. Hurricane Bob hit the island with a bang. The windows on Grandma and Grandpa's house rattled. The walls groaned. Every so often we'd hear a thud as something caught by the wind slammed into the side of the house. With the clouds, rain, wind, no electricity, and all the candles flickering, the house was really kind of spooky. Something in the back of my mind told me that if ever there was going to be a time for a ghost to show up, this was it. Sarah seemed to be thinking the same thing, so we both kept pretty close to Mom and Dad, Grandma and Grandpa.

For a long time we all just stared out the windows at the storm, but after a while we headed into the living room in the hope of keeping ourselves occupied as best we could without a television or a radio. Dad started to read with a flashlight. Mom began stitching on some needlework. Sarah and Grandma broke out the cribbage board, and Grandpa and I found the checkers board. Of course, much to my frustration, Grandpa kept beating me! And even though I knew I should be having fun playing a game with my grandfather, his winning all the time was starting to get on my nerves!

"Do you ever *lose*, Grandpa?" I finally

asked in an annoyed voice as he beat me one more time.

"Not very often," Grandpa admitted. "But your cousin Christopher beat me the last time he was visiting. And if Chris can beat me, so can you. Every time you visit you get a little bit better. It won't be long before you're the checkers champion of the house."

At that very moment there was a huge crash in the kitchen and the candle beside the checkers board suddenly blew out. I looked around in a panic to see if Sarah was thinking the same thing I was. Ghosts! Not again!

Grandma quickly jumped to her feet and scooted toward the noise. "Oh my *goodness*!" She bellowed. Sarah and I started to sink under our game tables for fear of what was coming next.

"Grandpa! You didn't shut the door all the way when you came in from outside. Now it's blown open and scared the wits out of me. You're in big trouble, buster!"

Of course today, Grandpa wasn't the only one who was going to be in trouble.

CHAPTER
5

After what seemed like the one-hundredth game of checkers, I finally beat Grandpa. As I did my victory dance I happened to look out the window and was thrilled to see a ray of sunshine breaking through the clouds.

"Look! The sun is coming out," I shouted.

"Well, sure enough," Grandma said. "It looks like Hurricane Bob has decided to move on and leave our island in peace."

As Sarah and I ran through the kitchen door and into the back yard, the wind was still blowing but it had quieted down a lot. The yard was a mess, with broken branches and leaves that had blown off the trees. When we ran to the front of the house to look down Main Street, we were surprised to see a big old elm tree had been pushed over and was actually leaning on a house.

"Ben, look at that tree," Sarah moaned. "If that house hadn't been there it would have fallen over completely."

"Sarah! Ben!" Dad called. "Let's help Grandpa get things out of the shop and the garage, and then we'll get ourselves out to Madaket to see if the cottage has blown away."

On the drive out to the cottage we didn't really see the effects of Hurricane Bob until we started to drive over Millie's Bridge and looked down Hither Creek.

"Look! There's a boat that's completely tipped over," Mom pointed out.

"And over there," Sarah blurted. "That boat has run aground."

"They must have broken loose from their moorings and then the wind and the waves took over," Dad added. "I know we would have been safe in the cottage, but hurricanes are dangerous. It was probably a good idea to go into town, just in case."

When we got to the cottage, the only thing that was even a little out of place was a piece of outdoor furniture that belonged to our neighbor. It had blown onto our porch. After Dad had returned it and we got everything out of the garage and back where it belonged, I asked Dad, "Can Sarah and I take a walk over to the surf?"

"Sure," Dad answered. "But stay away from the water. The waves will still be pounding and it's dangerous. I don't want you to even get your feet wet. Do you understand?"

"We understand," Sarah and I said together.

There was no doubt that Dad was right about the waves. We could hear them all the way to the path through the sand dunes.

"Do you think there'll be driftwood and stuff on the beach?" I wondered aloud.

"There'll either be a lot of it or the beach will be as clean as a whistle," Sarah answered. "It all depends on the tides and the wind."

"Maybe we'll find something interesting," I said with a grin.

Little did we know just how interesting and scary our discovery would be.

CHAPTER 6

"The beach looks so different!" Sarah gasped. "It's weird how a single storm can shift the sand around so much. Look! Where the beach used to be really wide, it's thin now. And over there, see how the waves washed all the way up to the sand dunes?"

"Yeah," I said. "And look at all the *stuff*!"

And sure enough, the beach was covered with the flotsam and jetsam of the ocean. There were branches, egg cartons, pieces of lumber, buoys, bottles, and old sneakers. There were tons of seaweed, not to mention an occasional beach chair and light bulb.

"Where does this stuff all come from?" I questioned.

"Who knows, Ben," Sarah answered. "It's just too bad that it all has to wash up here and mess up this beautiful beach."

"Yeah, it's too bad," I responded. "But it's kind of fun to beach comb…who knows what we might find."

As soon as the words were out of my mouth, I spotted what looked like a really old bottle.

"Hey Sarah," I shouted as I ran to my new treasure. "It's an old bottle with a cork in it."

"Not only that," Sarah said as she looked at the prize that I was now holding. "There's something in it that looks like a piece of paper!"

"Maybe it's a letter from an old sea captain," I joked.

But it was no joke, because finding that letter in the bottle was the beginning of another spooky adventure.

CHAPTER 7

"Pull the cork out, Ben." Sarah muttered as she tried to pry the bottle out of my hands.

"I'm trying. It's stuck," I groaned as I struggled with the cork. "Let me handle it Sarah, I found it—it's my bottle."

After a lot of wiggling and jiggling, the cork finally came free. I tipped the bottle upside down and managed to get a finger on the piece of paper inside.

"If I can just get it pressed up against the

glass, I think I can get it out. There! I've got
it," I said as I gently slid the piece of paper out
of the neck of the bottle.

The paper was rolled up and it looked
really old.

"Be careful unrolling it, Ben," Sarah
said.

"Give me a break, Sarah. I'm not stupid," I answered with a disgusted voice.

As I opened the paper we were amazed to see that it was a letter written in large flowing handwriting. And as we quickly scanned the paper, Sarah and I were horrified to see the signature at the bottom. The letter was signed "Captain Ichabod Paddack."

Sarah and I just stood and stared; we couldn't believe our eyes. We had met the ghost of Ichabod Paddack before on our visits to the island. The first time we had accidentally released him from an old sea chest and he had nearly swallowed our grandparents' house and us up in a nasty blue fog. The second time he had tried to force us to serve as his crew on his ghost ship and we had just barely escaped with our lives. We thought we were rid of him for good. But now here we were, holding a letter from him. And not only did he sign it, but it was addressed to us!

> Sarah and Ben,
> My dear little friends,
> You thought I was gone,
> My haunting at an end.
> My ship sails on,
> My ship sails free;
> A Nantucket sleighride
> Will bring you to me.
>
> Captain Ichabod Paddack

Sarah and I couldn't speak for a long time. We just stared at the letter. Finally, I asked, "What does he mean by a Nantucket sleighride?"

"I don't know," Sarah whispered aloud. "It's summer. There's no snow. What in the world is he talking about?"

"I have no idea," I grumbled. "But this

time we're staying out of Paddack's way. I've had it. No more spooks for me!"

If only I had been right.

CHAPTER
8

"Mom, Dad, what's a Nantucket sleigh-ride?" Sarah asked as we were sitting down to dinner back at the cottage.

"Now where in the world did you hear about that?" Dad wondered aloud before he launched into his explanation.

"Back in the whaling days, the ships were too big to get close enough to harpoon the whales. So the captain would lower small whaleboats. They were like long rowboats with ten or twelve men in them, like the one you saw at the whaling museum. Remember? One man would be up front in the bow with a harpoon connected to a really long rope. One man would be at the tiller in the back to steer, and the rest would row the boat. The whaleboats were fast and could get up close to the whales, and then the harpoon would be thrown. If it hit the whale and held fast, the whale— which was now hurt, frightened, and probably a little angry—would dive or start swimming away as fast as it could go. When the rope, which was fastened to the whaleboat, became tight, the whale would pull the whaleboat at breakneck speed through the water. That was a Nantucket sleighride.

"Finally, and this is the sad part, the whale would tire out and die. The whalemen would then pull the big creature back to the ship."

"So if somebody is on a Nantucket sleighride, they're hurting whales," Sarah said with a sad look in her eyes.

"Yes, Sarah. They are. It's not a pretty part of Nantucket's history, but it was a different time," Dad answered.

As I looked at Sarah I could tell that it wasn't Nantucket's history that she was worried about. It was Ichabod Paddack and what he was doing right now.

CHAPTER
9

Once dinner was over and the dishes were done, Sarah piped up, "Ben, how about we go down to the beach and watch the sunset?"

I knew by the sound of her voice that what she really wanted to do was talk about the letter we'd found in the bottle.

"Sure, Sarah, I'd be delighted," I said sarcastically.

To be honest, the last thing I wanted to do was talk about Ichabod Paddack and

Nantucket sleighrides. I didn't want to have anything to do with ghosts on this vacation. We'd done that before and I was tired of it. But sure enough, as soon as we got to the beach, my big sister started.

"Ben, we have to do something. Paddack is out there," she pleaded. "And he is going to hurt—no, he's going to *kill* some whales. We *have* to do something."

"And what are we going to do, Sarah?" I yelled as we walked along the beach. "How are we going to stop a ghost? We don't even know where he is. You know it's a big ocean. And even if we knew where he was, how would we get there?"

We walked along the shore in silence as the sun began to set. Then we stopped dead in our tracks. Not because of the beauty of the sunset, but because lying at our feet was another bottle, and in that bottle was another letter.

CHAPTER

10

"Sarah, don't open it," I begged. "Just throw it back in the water and let's forget all about it."

"No, Ben. We have to read the letter. Paddack is not going to leave us alone so we might as well just deal with him now and maybe somehow we'll be able to save some whales." And with that, Sarah pulled the cork from the bottle, fished out the letter from inside, and read it aloud:

At Georges Banks the humpbacks do sing.

To Georges Banks my harpoon I will
        bring.
A whaler I was,
A whaler I'll be;
A Nantucket sleighride
Is all I will need.

"Look, Ben, now we know where he'll be," Sarah said excitedly. "Georges Banks, wherever that is."

"Sarah, are you nuts? Even if we could find Georges Banks, how are we going to stop him?" I asked. "He's probably just trying to lure us out to the middle of nowhere so that he can get us onboard that ghost ship of his and force us to be his crew. We'd have to be nuts to go out there even if we could!"

"Believe me, I'll find a way," Sarah muttered with conviction. "Ichabod Paddack will not hurt another whale as long as I'm alive to stop him."

"That's my point, Sarah. That's exactly my point...as long as you're *alive*."

CHAPTER
11

Sarah and I didn't talk about Paddack or his letters any more that night as we took down the flag, played a few games of cribbage that of course I won, and then headed to bed.

But the next morning as we sat down to breakfast, Sarah suddenly asked, "Mom and Dad, do you know where Georges Banks are?"

I couldn't believe my ears. I absolutely couldn't believe that Sarah was asking this. I was sure that she had completely lost her mind.

Thankfully, Mom and Dad just looked at each other with blank expressions and slowly shook their heads.

"I've never heard of them, dear," Mom answered. "Are you talking about the kind of banks that you get money out of or the fishing banks that are out in the ocean?"

"The ocean kind," Sarah responded. "The places where you can find fish…and whales."

"I really don't have any idea," Dad added. "Maybe when we go to town you can ask Grandma and Grandpa. That sounds like something they might know."

"Okay," Sarah blurted. "Are we going in soon?"

"Whoa, what's your rush? We just sat down to breakfast," Mom countered.

"Yeah, what's your rush, Sarah?" I moaned.

"I'm just curious, that's all," she said with a determined look.

"Let's finish our breakfast," said Mom. "Then we can head into town. There are a few things I need to get at the store, and once we finish all our errands we can stop in and see Grandma and Grandpa."

"That'll be just fine," Sarah said, smiling.

As I looked at my sister, I just knew that all her questions were going to lead us into trouble.

CHAPTER 12

"So, what kind of errands do you have to run before we stop at Grandma and Grandpa's?" Sarah wondered aloud as Dad drove the Jeep into town.

"Well, we need to get some vegetables, so I thought we'd go out to the farm stand first," Mom said. "Then the grocery store for something for dinner, and since we'll be down at that end of town, we might as well stop at Island Marine and pick up a new American flag for the cottage. The Stars and Stripes we've been putting up every day is starting to fray badly and needs to be retired."

Slowly but surely, we made our way around to the different stores. With all the traffic it seemed to us kids that it was taking forever.

As we scooted down another side street, Dad said, "I tell you, when it comes to getting around Nantucket it sure helps to have grown up here and to know where all these little lanes go. I don't know how many more cars this island can handle!"

When at long last we pulled into Grandma and Grandpa's driveway on Main Street, Sarah was the first one out of the Jeep, and she quickly scampered into the house.

As I hurried in behind her, Sarah was shouting, "Hi Grandma! Hi Grandpa! Do you know where the Georges Banks are?"

"Now why in the world do you want to know that?" Grandma questioned.

"Sarah heard that there are whales there," I joined in.

"Well, I think you're right," Grandma nodded as she rubbed her chin. "The Georges Banks are quite a way off to the east of the island. They've long been known to be a spot with a lot of sea life, and this time of year there are a lot of humpback whales out there. In fact, if I remember right, there's a boat that leaves from Straight Wharf that takes people out to the Georges Banks for a whale watch. I'm pretty sure that I saw an ad for it in the *Inquirer and Mirror* the other day.

"Grandpa," Grandma called. "Is the *Inky Mirror* around somewhere?"

"Sure is. It's over here by my chair," Grandpa answered.

"Did you see an ad for a whale watch?"

"I think I did," Grandpa said as he picked up the paper and started searching for the ad. "Yup, here it is. It leaves at 8:30 in the morning from Straight Wharf. Why? Does somebody want to go?"

"You bet I do!" Sarah shouted, nearly jumping out of her skin. "And Ben does too! Don't you Ben?"

I just shook my head slowly and muttered, "If you say so, Sarah. If you say so."

CHAPTER
13

It didn't take a lot of convincing to get our parents to agree to go on the whale watch. Sarah found an ally in Grandma, who was sure that the trip would be "very educational." Mom looked at the ad in the newspaper and, after talking it over with Dad, called and made reservations for the four of us to go. What was funny though was that now that we were on our way to the Georges Banks, Sarah was suddenly very quiet. She didn't say a word all the way

back to Madaket or even during lunch. But once we all settled in at the beach, Sarah looked at me and said, "Ben, let's walk up to the Point."

"Gee, Sarah, I was just going to get the kite up. Couldn't we walk later?" I whined.

"No, Ben. I'd like to go for a walk NOW!" she demanded.

I knew that Sarah had something up her sleeve, and I was pretty sure I knew what it was.

We were just about halfway to Smith's Point when Sarah finally asked, "Ben, will you help me tomorrow?"

"Help you what?"

"Stop Ichabod Paddack from hurting any more whales."

"Sarah, we don't even know if we're going to see Paddack," I roared. "We don't know where exactly he'll be or when he'll be there. The Georges Banks must cover hundreds of miles of ocean…thousands, maybe."

"Yes, but we're going where the whales are and I'm sure he'll be there too," Sarah answered. "If we see him, will you help me?"

At first I didn't know what to say, but then I looked into my big sister's worried eyes and I knew I had to help her. "Sarah, I told you when we found the first letter that I didn't want to have anything to do with him again. But I've been thinking about it since we found that second letter in the bottle. I don't know how we'll do it, but I'll help, not just to stop him from hurting the whales but also to stop him from haunting us. So now that we've settled that, let's enjoy our day at the beach."

"Thank you, Ben," Sarah said as she smiled and began running. "Race you to the Point!"

Of course I ran after her. There was no way I could let my sister beat me in a race! But just when I was about to catch up, she stopped dead in her tracks.

"Sarah!" I yelled as I almost ran into her. "What's the matter? Why did you stop?"

And then I saw what was lying in front of her on the beach. It was another bottle with a letter inside.

As she stood frozen, I picked up the bottle, saying, "We need to read it." I pulled out the cork and managed to fish out the letter.

Unrolling the paper, I read the words aloud:

> Sarah and Benjamin, my dear little
>   friends,
> At Georges Banks we'll at last meet
>   again.
> A Nantucket sleighride, the excitement
>   you'll see.
> On a Nantucket sleighride, my crew you
>   will be.
> Tomorrow's the day.
> Rest well in your bed.
> By this time tomorrow a whale will be
>   dead.

I looked at Sarah, and when our eyes met I said, "I don't know how we're going to do it, Sarah, but we've got to stop him for good."

CHAPTER
14

The next morning we woke up at the crack of dawn and got ourselves ready for what promised to be an exciting day. Mom made sandwiches, collected snacks, and packed everything in a cooler for the trip. Dad was having a great time making sure all his camera equipment was ready for a day of picture-taking. Sarah and I fidgeted our way through breakfast and couldn't help but wonder what the rest of the day would bring.

"Okay, let's get ourselves ready and load

up the Jeep," Dad finally said as he picked up Sadie's leash. "Sadie, you're going to stay with Grandma and Grandpa today. We're going on an adventure."

Sadie wagged her tail as she headed out the door behind Dad.

"Did everybody bring a sweatshirt, a sweater, or a jacket?" Mom asked as we piled into the car. "The person I spoke to on the phone when I made the whale-watch reservation said to be sure to bring something warm, because it's usually a good 20 degrees cooler out on the water."

"I think we have everything," Dad answered, and with that we were on our way.

We parked the Jeep at Grandma and Grandpa's house, said our goodbyes to Sadie, and then walked downtown to Straight Wharf lugging our cooler, coats, sweatshirts, and Dad's camera equipment. Sarah and I were both excited and scared as we walked. It was exciting to think we would be seeing whales out in the ocean. It was scary to know that we might also encounter Ichabod Paddack again, but we knew that it was something we had to do not just to save the whales, but hopefully to save ourselves from Paddack haunting us forever.

CHAPTER
15

"Here we go," Sarah said as the crew of the *Whale Watch 2* cast off the lines holding the ship to the dock.

Slowly but surely we picked up speed and began to move into Nantucket harbor. The ship was really nice. There was a good-sized cabin with a snack bar and a lot of seating for passengers inside. Outside there was a walkway around the entire ship with plenty of space in the bow where people could stand and watch for whales. If you wanted to sit outside, there was built in seating along the side of the cabin that was great—as long as you didn't mind getting a little wet when the waves splashed up as the ship was under way. If you wanted to get a better view, there was also a place up on the top deck where you could scan the whole horizon. The weather was perfect. The morning sun was warm and the sky was clear as we rounded Brant Point and headed for the end of the Jetties, where the captain turned eastward.

"Good morning, this is your captain speaking. I'd like to welcome you aboard the *Whale Watch 2*. Today we will be making our way to the Georges Banks, and it is our hope that we will see a wide range of sea life. Please understand that we cannot guarantee you will see whales today. It's a big ocean. But with our experience, our radar, and radio communication with fishing boats on the Banks, we have an outstanding record of giving our passengers an exciting day of whale sightings. On our trips we have regularly spotted Atlantic white-sided dolphins, Minke whales, right whales and the ever-popular humpbacks. When we spot sea life, we will point it out to you by using the ship like a giant clock. If I announce that we have sighted something at 12 o'clock, that means you should look straight ahead toward the bow. If I tell you there is a whale at 3 o'clock, then please look to the starboard or the right side of the ship. Nine o'clock is to the port or left side of the ship, and so on. Now, please sit back and enjoy the cruise. I'm sure we will have an exciting and unforgettable day."

With all my doubts and fears, that was one thing I was sure about. Today would be exciting, unforgettable, and probably scary, too.

CHAPTER
16

The morning passed quickly as we made our way toward the Georges Banks. True to the captain's word, we saw all kinds of sea life. At one point the captain slowed the ship to point out what he called a "megapod" of Atlantic white-sided dolphins. There were a lot of them. It was fun to see them skimming just under the surface on either side of the bow. Every so often they'd jump out of the water in a beautiful arc and then disappear again as they made a perfect dive back into the water.

Later on we heard the captain announce, "Folks, if you'll look to 2 o'clock, we're coming up on what appears to be a right whale with a calf. We've spotted this pair several times on our cruises. You'll notice that when they submerge they don't curve their backs and splash their tails like the humpbacks. That's because they don't need the force of the tail to push them down. Rather, the right whales, when they want to dive, simply submerge just like a submarine."

It was cool to see the whales, and we kept up with the mother and calf for a while. Dad was having a great time with his camera and was taking a lot of pictures.

Mom seemed to be enjoying the cruise as much as I was and even Sarah, who still seemed a little nervous about running into

Captain Paddack, looked thrilled to see the whales.

Suddenly, the captain increased the speed of the ship and announced, "We are now approaching Georges Banks. At 12 o'clock we have just spotted a humpback whale breaching the surface. For those of you not familiar with the term, breaching is when a whale jumps

right out of the water. We'll be there in just a couple of minutes and hopefully the whales will give you all a wonderful show."

And give us a show they did. The captain slowed the ship and we could hardly believe our luck. "Folks, right now there are so many whales around us that I don't even need to tell you where to look. Just open your eyes and look in any direction. We have at least fifteen humpbacks who have all come for a visit."

He was right. Everywhere we looked, we could see a whale either surfacing and spouting or arching its back and flipping up its tail to dive down into the deeps. Once, a humpback started swimming directly toward our ship as if it was going to ram us, but then it dove under the boat. A few minutes later, a whale breached right beside our ship, and when it landed back in the water everybody on that side of the boat was soaked to the skin by the splash!

I couldn't believe that Sarah and I had found our way to Georges Banks. Whales surrounded us. The only question was, where was Ichabod Paddack?

Unfortunately, it didn't take long to find out.

CHAPTER 17

Sarah and I were so involved watching the whales that we were surprised when the captain announced, "Folks, it looks like the show's coming to an end for today. We've got a fog bank moving in on us from the east, and it's moving fast."

When I looked up I was shocked to see the bow of our ship disappearing into the fog.

"Whoa, Sarah, look at the fog," I whispered. "Can you believe how thick it is?"

"I believe it, Ben." Sarah groaned.

"Remember the other times we ran into Paddack. It was foggy then, too."

Sarah was right. Every time we had encountered Paddack's ghost there'd been this creepy blue fog, and here we were surrounded by it again. But what was even spookier was that when the fog shrouded the ship, the engines shut down and everybody except Sarah and I disappeared. One minute we were part of a crowd of people watching the whales and the next, everybody was gone.

"Mom! Dad! Where are you?" Sarah shouted.

We quickly ran the length of the ship... nobody. We scampered up the stairs to the viewing deck...nobody.

And then we heard a horrible voice calling to us out of the fog:

Sarah and Ben my dear little friends,
Your journey to find me has come to an
        end.
Take up the oars as part of my crew—
The ride of your lives I will give to you.
A whaler I was,
A whaler I'll be;
A Nantucket sleighride is all that I'll
        need.

"No, Paddack!" I screamed at the top of my lungs. "We'll never help you kill a whale. Not as long as there's a breath in our bodies."

Sarah and I huddled together on the deck of the *Whale Watch 2*, shaking in fear and defiance, when the voice called back from the fog.

Sarah and Ben, my brave little crew,
There's really no reason for me to hurt
        you.
Row my oars,
Give me my thrill,
Or it's more than a whale I'll be forced
        to kill.

As we listened to the voice from the fog, the two of us moved closer to the railing to see if we could catch a glimpse of Ichabod Paddack. But instead of Captain Paddack, what we saw was a huge old whaling ship at full sail coming straight for the *Whale Watch 2*. It hit our ship with a crunch and the force of the collision threw Sarah and me over the side.

At first we sank beneath the surface, but as we kicked for dear life our heads broke the water and we gasped for a breath of fresh air. Thankfully, we came up right beside what looked like a long, sleek rowboat and we quickly grabbed the gunwales and pulled ourselves to safety. The only problem was that when we wiped the water from our eyes Sarah and I found ourselves staring at the terrible ghost of Captain Ichabod Paddack.

CHAPTER
18

Sarah and I sat side by side on the center seat of the whaleboat with our hands on the oars. We didn't want to help Paddack, but what else could we do? We were all by ourselves in the middle of the Atlantic with nobody to help us. I'd never dreamed that we would find ourselves in so much trouble. Sarah looked totally overwhelmed. She just stared down at her feet and sniffled back the tears.

"Sarah, don't worry," I whispered. "We'll get out of this somehow. I promise."

"I never should have talked you into coming out here in the first place," she mumbled. "Why did I ever think we could stop a ghost from hurting whales?"

"We came out here because we both thought it was the right thing to do," I said in a low voice.

Paddack, who was now standing in the bow of the boat with his harpoon, turned to us again.

Ah, my children, my Sarah and Ben,
No need to cry or whisper again.
Do my bidding, the oars are for you—
We'll hunt whales together,
Just me and you two.

"I guess we'd better start rowing," I groaned. "Who knows—maybe we'll row ourselves back to the island."

Sarah and I strained at the oars. It was a good thing the ocean was calm, because the whaleboat really needed about ten strong men to move it quickly through the water.

"I don't think we have to worry about catching up with a whale the way we're rowing," I whispered to my sister.

"Yeah, but Paddack's an experienced whaler," Sarah answered. "He may be evil, but he's smart. The whales aren't expecting any danger. He'll probably just use us to maneuver the whaleboat to a place where he thinks a whale will surface, and then he'll strike."

"I hate to admit it, Sarah, but I think you're right. Look, he's getting ready to throw his harpoon."

And sure enough, Captain Paddack was standing in the bow of the boat holding his harpoon like a spear. Then, without warning, he let it fly, shouting:

Thar she blows!
Let her rip.
A Nantucket sleighride
Is a wonderful trip.

Paddack had thrown his harpoon just as a giant humpback had surfaced and spouted. The harpoon's point, which was shaped like an arrowhead, had hit the back of the whale and it held fast. It didn't look as if it was really secure, but at least for now it was holding. The whale was definitely upset and immediately started to dive. A long rope that was fastened to the harpoon was coiled up in the bow and it started to quickly play out into the water after the whale. When the rope pulled tight, the whaleboat suddenly jerked to full speed. Besides the sound of the whaleboat skimming the water, all Sarah and I could hear was the sound of Ichabod Paddack's piercing cry:

> Hang on, my children, grab hold of your
> seats!
> A Nantucket sleighride is a whaler's
> great treat.

We were now in for the ride of our lives. We just hoped that it wasn't the end for both the whale and us.

CHAPTER
19

Our whaleboat traveled across the ocean's surface at breakneck speed. It had only been a matter of minutes, but it seemed like hours, and I was sure the whale had pulled us miles from the *Whale Watch 2*. Paddack was howling in delight, when all of a sudden the whale breached from the water ahead of us As it twisted its body and fell back into the sea, I spotted the harpoon falling free.

"The harpoon came loose!" I shouted.

Captain Paddack looked as if he'd just

been hit with a ton of bricks. He collapsed in the bow of the boat holding his head and moaning.

> The whale is lost,
> My harpoon came free.
> What in creation will become of me?
> We'll hunt again; a whale will be mine.
> We'll hunt again; my aim will be fine.

Then he looked at us and scowled, saying, "Row, children, row."

And that's exactly what we did, but as the whaleboat started to move, Sarah and I saw a humpback whale that seemed to be swimming in giant circles around our boat. Each time it went around us it gained speed and came closer and closer. Finally, it swam way ahead of us, turned around, and almost stopped in the water. And then, to our horror, it headed straight for our whaleboat.

Paddack had seen the whale too, and was frantically pulling on the rope connected to his harpoon, trying to get his hands on his weapon to strike the whale again. But the rope was too long and the whale was too fast.

"Ben, when I say jump, jump for your life!" Sarah gasped as the whale seemed to pick up even more speed. "It's better to be in the water when it hits than in the boat. One, two, three, JUMP!"

We both hit the water at the same time just as the whale struck the boat. As the huge creature passed under the now broken hull, it flipped its tail, shattering what was left of the boat to pieces. The ghost of Ichabod Paddack was thrown into the air and then slowly glided down to the sea. All the while he moaned.

My ship is gone,
My tears I will shed.

The sea is my home,
I'll now rest with the dead.

And with that, his ghostly image faded from sight.

Sarah and I watched as Ichabod Paddack disappeared before our eyes.

"Is he really gone?" I wondered aloud.

"I don't know for sure, Ben," Sarah answered. "I think without a ship he's gone forever. There's only one problem now."

"What's that, Sarah?" I asked.

"How long can you dog-paddle?"

But before I could answer, the humpback whale, which moments before had crushed Paddack's whaleboat, now surfaced gently between us and held out its flukes for us to grab.

"Do you think he knows we didn't want to hurt him?" I questioned.

"Who knows, but right now he or *she* is our only hope," Sarah answered.

And with the gentle flick of its tail, the whale started to float along the ocean's surface to the west and, much to our relief, a few minutes later we spotted the *Whale Watch 2*.

The fog was just lifting when the humpback left us close to our ship. It simply flipped its tail again and dove down deep, leaving us to make the rest of the way on our own.

As the fog disappeared, we could see Mom and Dad on the deck of the *Whale Watch 2* frantically scanning the water along with the rest of the passengers.

"There they are!" Mom shouted when she spotted us. "Sarah and Ben, thank goodness you're safe!" she cried as we slowly climbed up a rope ladder that the crew had lowered for us. "How in the world did you fall overboard?"

"Believe me, Mom," I answered as the crew wrapped us in blankets. "You wouldn't believe us if we told you."

CHAPTER
20

The next afternoon, the whole family was strolling up Madaket beach toward Smith's Point. Sarah and I were both pretty quiet, because we were thinking a lot about everything that had happened out on the Georges Banks.

Dad had brought a tennis ball along and kept throwing it ahead of us so that Sadie would chase after it instead of the seagulls. The beach still had a lot of flotsam and jetsam left over from Hurricane Bob. But Sarah and I really didn't have much interest. We were just happy to look for pieces of quahog shells that had been polished by the sea and the sand.

Sadie lost interest in Dad's tennis ball and ran way ahead of us, and then all of a sudden she picked something up and trotted back toward us.

"Now, what in the world did she find?" Dad asked no one in particular. "I hope it's not some smelly old fish."

But as Sadie came closer, we saw that it wasn't a fish she was carrying in her mouth. It was an old bottle, just like the ones we had found before with the letters from Ichabod Paddack. Sadie trotted right up to Sarah and me and dropped it at our feet. It was the same kind of bottle, all right. There was even a cork in it. But this time there was no letter.

Sarah and I just stared at the bottle until finally, my sister picked it up.

"Why on earth would Sadie bring you an old bottle?" Mom questioned. "It's too bad there's not a letter in it. That would be exciting."

I took the bottle from Sarah's hand, and side by side we walked over to the edge of the surf. With a running start, I threw that bottle out into the water as far as I could.

Then Sarah and I looked at each other, shook our heads, and said together, "We've had enough excitement for this vacation. Let's just walk to the Point."

Look for more spooky tales by

Warren Hussey Bouton

Sea Chest
in the Attic

The Ghost
on Main Street

The Ghost
of Ichabod Paddack

and

Oliver's
Ghost

For information about Hither Creek Press
or to contact the author send your email to:
Hithercreekpress@aol.com